Roxie

Loves Adventure

*To Roxie, who brings love, glamour,
and pug fur to everything she touches
—S.B-Q.*

*For Roxie and all her
cute puggy-ness, and for
Sudipta—the ten-year wait
was worth it, my friend!
—L.H.*

ISBN 978-1-339-03205-4

Text © 2022 Sudipta Bardhan-Quallen. Illustrations © 2022 Leeza Hernandez.
All rights reserved. Published by Scholastic Inc., 557 Broadway, New York, NY 10012,
by arrangement with Abrams Books for Young Readers, an imprint of ABRAMS.
SCHOLASTIC and associated logos are trademarks and/or registered trademarks of Scholastic Inc.

12 11 10 9 8 7 6 5 4 3 2 1   23 24 25 26 27 28

Printed in the U.S.A.   40

First Scholastic printing, September 2023

Book design by Heather Kelly

The illustrations and textures in this book were rendered by hand
with paint, pencil, and ink, then collaged together in Photoshop.

Roxie
Loves Adventure

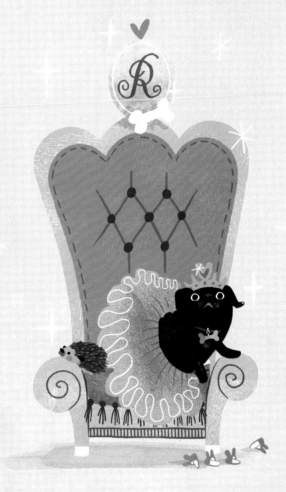

Written by

Sudipta Bardhan-Quallen

Illustrated by

Leeza Hernandez

SCHOLASTIC INC.

Roxie was a pug with style,
Both elegant and classy.
She lounged upon her throne and smiled,
So happy, spoiled, and gassy.

Her treats were kept on hand all day,
Displayed on silver dishes.
Her humans let her have her way.
They saw to all her wishes.

Pugs like her were meant to be

INDULGED,

ADORED,

and **SNUGGLED.**

She was made for luxury—
She wasn't built to struggle.

One day, Roxie woke at dawn,
She needed . . . well, you know.

Her humans were still snoring on,
But she just had to *go*.

She spied a spot behind a bush,
Soon Roxie felt relief.

But when she gave the door a push,
She stopped in disbelief.

It wouldn't move, no matter how

She **SHOVED** or **BUMPED** or **BUCKED.**

Soon, sweat was beading on her brow.

She scowled and shouted . . .

How long would she be trapped outdoors?

Her humans couldn't help.

Roxie heard their distant snores.

"I'm on my own!" she yelped.

No bed! No bowl! No ball! No treat!

No daily manicure!

No fuzzy slippers for her feet!

How could a pug endure?

Desperate to escape the **WILD,**

She looked for some way back.

She spied a window and she smiled—

Her humans left it **CRACKED!**

But pugs were never built to jump!
Their legs were far too stumpy.
She tried, but landed on her rump—
Her failure made her grumpy.

Just then, a mail truck crossed the road,
And Roxie knew for sure
That there'd be boxes to unload—
Perhaps an open door?

But pugs were never built for speed!
The truck soon backed away.
Her racing skills could not succeed,
Especially not today!

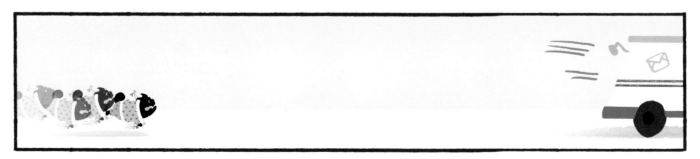

Roxie slumped down in the grass,
Accepting she had failed.
She spied her humans through the glass—
That's when she heard them wail!

ROXIE?

TREATS!

ROXIE!

"They need me!"
Roxie finally saw.
"I must find some
way back!"

She pushed the boxes with a paw
And saw how they were stacked.

Though pugs were never built to climb,
That didn't mean a thing!
She would not quit! No, not this time!
"I'll give that bell a ring!"

The first box wasn't all that bad.
She pulled herself up quickly.

The second one made Roxie sad—

The third one left her sickly.

But nothing would prevent this pup
From summiting that tower!
Just one more box! She clambered up
With her last ounce of power.

As Roxie's strength was failing.
Her effort was supremely timed—
Soon, she fell over, flailing.

PLOP!

OOF!

Roxie could not quite recall
Whatever happened next.
She woke confused, about to bawl,
But then grew quite perplexed.

She was no longer in the wild
But *home* with all her stuff.
Filled with pride, she sweetly smiled—
She'd proven pugs are tough.

Then fizzy drinks and tasty treats
Were served at Roxie's pleasure.
With fuzzy slippers on her feet,
She felt both loved and treasured.

PFFT!

She nestled into bed that night,
Her heart filled with elation.
The world outside held no more fright
And needed exploration!

Pugs like her were meant to be
Indulged—that much was true.
She was made for luxury,
But for adventure, too.

Roxie rose before the dawn.
She leaped up out of bed!

ZZZz

Her humans were still snoring on.
"I don't need them!" she said.

She'd face whatever came her way,

From **SNAKES**

to **WOLVES**

to **BEARS.**

"I know that I'll be brave today—
But first . . .

. . . what will I wear?"

Sudipta Bardhan-Quallen splits her time between managing Foxy Roxie the Pug's social media and writing children's books, which include *Tyrannosaurus Wrecks!*, *Quackenstein Hatches a Family*, and *Chicks Rule!* Sudipta and Roxie live in New Jersey with a grumble comprised of a human adult husband and three human children, all of whom are markedly less glamorous and disappointingly unfurry.

Leeza Hernandez is a British designer and illustrator who spends most of her time drawing animals and human children. She is best known for her work on the Mia Mayhem book series and on *New York Times* bestselling author John Lithgow's *Never Play Music Right Next to the Zoo*. Leeza currently resides in Florida with her own adult human husband and human child, along with her cats, Jaspurr and Princess Pippa. She has also attempted to befriend the baby alligator in the lake behind her house but with little success . . . yet!